How the CRAYONS Saved the RAINBOW

For Amanda and Shirley. -M. S.

For Lesley. -F. P. T.

How the Crayons Saved the RAINBOW

Written by Monica Sweeney
Illustrated by Feronia Parker Thomas

SCHOLASTIC INC.

The Sun and the Clouds were best friends.
They worked together to keep the earth warm and gardens growing.

But of all the things they did together, their very favorite was making rainbows so that the whole world was colorful and happy.

Then one day, the Sun and the Clouds had a big fight.
The Clouds were blocking the Sun, and the Sun
couldn't shine through to the Earth.

The Sun went *sizzle sizzle sizzle!* at the Clouds, and the
Clouds went *clap bang boom!* back.

They stopped being friends and were never in the sky together again.

With the Sun and Clouds far apart, it was scorching hot on some days . . .

and damp and cold on others.

And worst of all, there were no more rainbows! Without rainbows, the flowers, streams, and even cities started to lose their color.

Soon, the Earth was black and white.

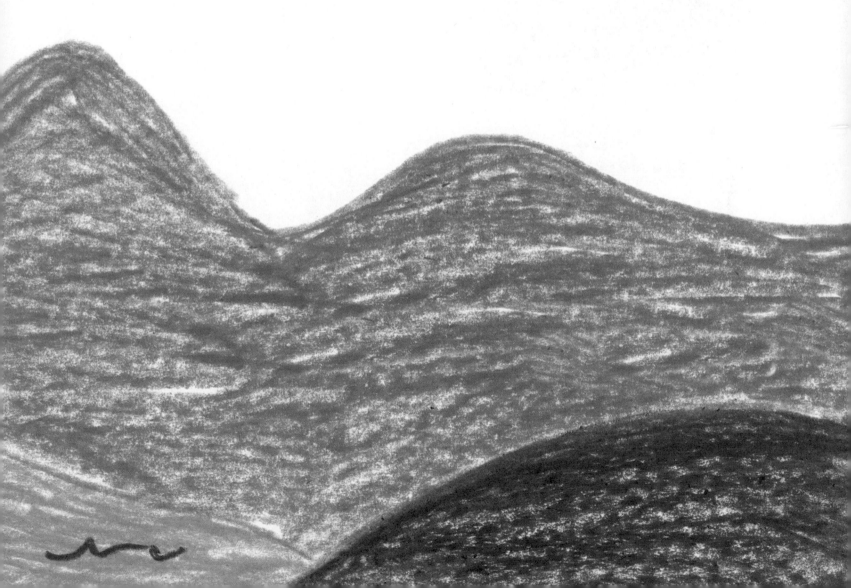

But in one little town, in one little school, in one little desk,
there was one little forgotten box of crayons.
And the crayons still had their colors.

The desk rattled, shook, clambered, and clanked.

All of a sudden, it toppled over and the box of crayons tumbled out!

The crayons started to search for the colors. They raided marker bins and tore through art projects, but everything as far as they could see was only black and white.

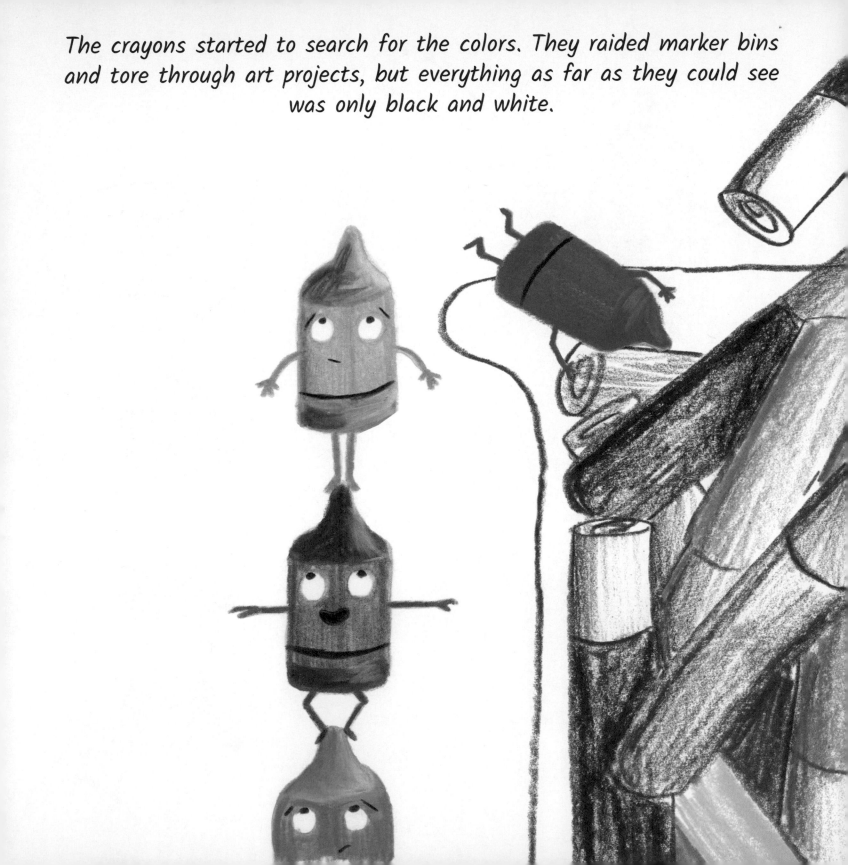

The crayons looked out the window.
The Sun was all the way to one side of the sky looking angry,
and the Clouds were all the way to the other looking gloomy.

So the crayons started drawing little rainbows all over town.

But nothing happened. The Sun and the Clouds didn't seem to notice.

"We have to make our rainbows bigger!" Violet said.
Working together, the crayons drew and scribbled.

They made the biggest, brightest, most colorful rainbow the world had ever seen!

Ever so slowly, the Sun perked up,
and the Clouds floated in
for a closer look.

The Sun and the Clouds both
peered down, admiring the
giant rainbow that the crayons
had drawn.

"What bright colors!" said the Sun.
"It's incredible!" said the Clouds.

They looked at each other with
great big smiles.

The Sun said to the Clouds,
"Remember when we used to be
together all the time and make rainbows?"

The Clouds nodded.
"I'm sorry for going **clap bang boom!** at you."
"I'm sorry for going *sizzle sizzle sizzle!* at you,"
said the Sun.

"It's better being friends!" said the Sun, and the Clouds agreed.
They hugged. The Sun shined brightly and the Clouds misted happy rain.
Ever so slowly, rainbows reappeared near and far,
turning the world colorful once again.

ISBN 978-1-338-26190-5

18 17 16   21 22

Printed in the U.S.A.   40

First Scholastic printing, November 2017

Cover design and illustration by Feronia Parker Thomas
Special thanks to Monica Sweeney and Feronia Parker Thomas